Billy Burger
MODEL CITIZEN

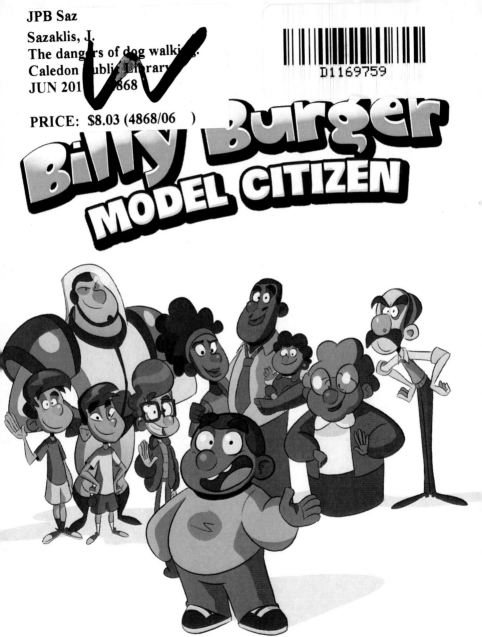

CALEDON PUBLIC LIBRARY

Billy Burger, Model Citizen is published by
Stone Arch Books,
A Capstone Imprint
1710 Roe Crest Drive
North Mankato, Minnesota 56003
www.mycapstone.com

Library of Congress Cataloging-in-Publication Data
Sazaklis, John, author.
  The dangers of dog walking / by John Sazaklis ; illustrated by Lee Robinson.
     pages cm. — (Billy Burger, model citizen)
  Summary: When third-grader Billy Burger gets into a fight with Randy, the school bully, he is
suspended, and his parents, while sympathetic, assign him to volunteer for the Shake-a-paw
Animal Shelter, which is not so bad, except for the dog poop—and proves to have unexpected
benefits when Randy corners him in an alley.
  ISBN 978-1-4965-2587-1 (library binding)
  ISBN 978-1-4965-2684-7 (paperback.)
  ISBN 978-1-4965-2688-5 (eBook)
1. Bullies—Juvenile fiction. 2. Animal shelters—Juvenile fiction. 3. Dogs—Juvenile fiction.
4. Voluntarism—Juvenile fiction. 5. Families—Juvenile fiction. 6. Elementary schools—Juvenile
fiction. [1. Bullying—Fiction. 2. Animal shelters—Fiction. 3. Dogs—Fiction. 4. Voluntarism—
Fiction. 5. Family life—Fiction. 6. Schools—Fiction.] I. Robinson, Lee (Illustrator), illustrator.
II. Title.

PZ7.S27587Dan 2016
813.6—dc23 [Fic]   2015032131

Illustrations by: Lee Robinson
Book design by: Ted Williams
Photo credit: Happy Animals Club, page 94

Printed and bound in the United States of America
009745R

Billy Burger
MODEL CITIZEN

THE DANGERS
OF DOG WALKING

BY JOHN SAZAKLIS

STONE ARCH BOOKS
a capstone imprint

TABLE OF CONTENTS

HEY, WHAT'S UP?

MY NAME IS
BILLY BURGER.

Nice to meet you! If you're reading this, you have good taste in books. Now that I know something about you, how about I tell you something about me?

I live with my family in a medium-sized house, in a little town called Hicksville, in the big state of New York. Our medium-sized house got much smaller the same time my family got a little bigger—when my baby sister, Ruby, was born. She's kind of cute . . . if you like stinky, smelly, noisemakers!

My parents both work at the Hicksville Police Department. Pretty cool, huh? Dad is a detective. Mom is a criminal psychologist. Together, they solve mysteries and catch troublemakers. Now that I think about it, that isn't much different than taking care of me!

But I wouldn't call myself a troublemaker, exactly. I prefer the term *adventurer*. I'm always looking for interesting things to do or discover because I get bored easily. I think it's because I have an overactive imagination.

(Want to know what's more overactive than my imagination? My appetite! I love to eat, and sometimes I think about that more than anything else. Seriously. I'll try anything . . . twice!)

I usually don't go on adventures alone. My partner in crime is also my best friend, Teddy. He lives a few houses down from me on the same block. I'm always trying to think of fun things for us to do together!

When I get an idea it is usually awesomely epic. Unfortunately, my ideas don't always go as planned, and that's when I get in trouble.

But I'm working on that.

I'm working on being a better person, a better student, a better everything. Just like my grandpa, William Burger—the Hero of Hicksville. He's sort of a legend in our town. He did good deeds and inspired others to do the same.

And like Grandpa, I'm going to do just that.

I'm going to become **BILLY BURGER: MODEL CITIZEN!**

1
Out of This World

"Last one there is a rotten dinosaur egg!" Teddy cries.
He sprints off the bus and runs into the school.

"Oh, man!" I shout and race after him.

Teddy runs everywhere. Meanwhile, running is one
of my least favorite things to do. I think it should be
saved for real emergencies, like being chased by a pack of
zombies or real dinosaurs.

But I also don't like losing, so I sprint as fast as I can to
catch up.

When Teddy reaches the front entrance, he leans on
the door and looks at his watch.

When I reach the door, I'm winded and trying to catch my breath.

"Hey, Billy," Teddy says. "What took you so long? Did you stop to feed the birds along the way?"

"Ha-ha," I say. "Not all of us had gazelle food for breakfast."

Teddy scrunches his nose. "What's that smell?" he asks. "Oh, right, it's a **ROTTEN** dinosaur egg!"

He points at me and laughs.

"You're lucky you're my best friend," I tell him. "Because if I were a dinosaur, I'd chew you up and spit out your bones."

"Well, that's a rotten thing to do," Teddy says with a smile.

"What did you expect?" I reply. "I hatched from a rotten dinosaur egg!"

The two of us laugh and high-five. Then we walk to our classroom.

Teddy and I are both in Mr. Karas's third-grade class here at Fork Lane School. I really like the name because it makes me think of eating food.

And that makes me think of lunch.

And sometimes I spend the entire morning staring at the clock, waiting for it to be lunchtime.

But when I'm not hungry or thinking about food, I like listening to Mr. Karas teach. Mr. Karas is a tall man with a beard. He brings in his guitar and sings songs that help us learn. He's goofy but cool and fun at the same time.

As the kids pile into the room, Mr. Karas claps his hands together and says, "Good morning, class! Once you're settled and hand in your homework, I am going to tell you about our next exciting scientific adventure. You could say it is . . . out of this world!"

"But is it something cool?" I call out.

"Billy, that's a warning, young man," Mr. Karas says as he writes my name on the board. "You know you have to raise your hand to ask a question, right?"

OH, MAN! Now I have a warning. That's like strike one. Two more strikes and I'm out—out of the classroom and headed straight down to Principal Crank's office.

"Sorry, sir. I forgot," I say. I just get so excited about adventure that I can't contain myself.

Grumpily, I take out my homework from my schoolbag and hand it in.

Back at my desk, I lean over and say to Teddy, "Do you think we'll do something cool like dissect frogs?"

Teddy shrugs. "My older brother didn't get to cut open a frog until high school. So, probably not," he says.

"SAY WHAT?!" I exclaim. "High school? I can't wait that long."

"Yuck," says a high-pitched voice behind us. It's Polly.

Polly Pembroke is the class know-it-all. She's also kind of a snob.

"Frogs are slimy and gross," she says.

I try to say something clever, but she may actually be right.

"Hey, Teddy, frogs *are* slimy. How do you get them to stay still before you dissect them? Aren't they slippery and hopping all over the place?"

"The frogs are already dead," says Polly. "They're soaked in formaldehyde."

Teddy and I look at each other.

"You mean the stuff that is in toothpaste?" he asks.

"No, that's fluoride," she says. "Formaldehyde is an embalming agent."

We stare at her.

She replies very slowly. "That means . . . it keeps the dead bodies fresh . . . so they don't rot and decay."

"Just like the stuff in toothpaste!" Teddy exclaims.

"Yeah!" I cry.

Polly rolls her eyes and lets out a deep sigh. Then she flips her hair and ignores us.

Teddy and I look at each other and shrug. Girls. We'll never understand them.

All of a sudden, Teddy looks deep in thought.

"What is it?" I ask.

"I'm wondering if I should have saved my baby teeth and put them in formaldehyde," he says. "I'll start doing it with the next one!"

I wonder the same thing until Mr. Karas interrupts my thoughts.

"Today's scientific journey will take us beyond the classroom, beyond the moon, and into our solar system!" he says.

"YESSS!" Teddy and I whisper to each other.

We love stuff about outer space.

We both have books about the planets and constellations.

We both build model rocket ships from scratch.

And we both love the cartoon *Super Samurai from Outer Space*!

Mr. Karas pulls up an image of the solar system on the smartboard. Then he walks across the room and turns off the lights.

In the dark, the colors of the planets and the Sun look bright and real. It feels like we're floating in between them.

"There is so much about our universe that we know and so much more that we don't know," Mr. Karas says.

The teacher tells us how the names of the planets and their moons came from Greek and Roman mythology.

Most of it is stuff I already know from my books and
favorite cartoon, but it's nice to hear it again.

Mr. Karas picks up his guitar and says, "Now I'm going
to sing a song from a television program I watched when I
was your age."

He strums a few chords and begins to sing.

The closest to the Sun, is the planet Mercury,

Then the shrouded planet Venus is as gassy as can be.

The Earth is next, we call it home, let's hope it stays
  that way,

And then there's Mars, it's really red, what more can I say?

The song is really catchy and I tap my foot along with the beat. Then I look up at the wall, see the clock, and gasp.

Whoa! I think to myself. *Time does fly when you're having fun.*

Before I blurt out the teacher's name, I stop myself and remember to raise my hand.

Mr. Karas stops singing and says, "Yes, Billy? Is it something urgent?"

"It most certainly is!" I say, pointing at the clock. "It's lunchtime!"

2
SPACE RACE

"It *is* lunchtime," Mr. Karas says. "I got so caught up in our lesson that I forgot to watch the time."

"It's all right, Mr. Karas," I tell him. "Just don't let it happen again."

The teacher smiles at me and shakes his head.

"Before we line up for lunch, here's some food for thought," he says. "I want each of you to pair up with a friend and create an arts-and-crafts project based on our solar system. The sky's the limit!"

While Mr. Karas puts his guitar into its case, I blast out of my chair like a rocket ship! **ZOOM!**

Teddy does the same and says, "Last one to the cubbies has to share his treat!"

And like that, he's gone in the blink of an eye.

Nothing in the world is going to make me share my food. **ESPECIALLY** my treat. That's the best part!

I hustle after my best friend, but Teddy's got speed.

Luckily for me, he's also careless and clumsy. And since he never ties his shoelaces, he trips over them and tumbles to the ground. **BAM!**

I jump over Teddy and reach the cubbies first.

"Victory is mine!" I shout.

I hold up my lunch box like a gold trophy.

Teddy grumpily hands me his bag of chocolate chunk cookies.

"Thank you very much," I say and drop it into my lunch box.

Then I have a change of heart.

"I'll tell you what, Teddy," I say to my best friend. "You get to keep the cookies on a technicality, but learn to tie those laces!"

Once we get to the cafeteria, Teddy and I work our way through the maze of kids. We look for our friends Michael and Jason, but we also keep an eye out for Randy.

Randy is a bully, and we've started calling him Randy the Savage.

As if picking on us on the bus isn't enough, he tries to steal our lunch money, too. Luckily, his ugly mug is nowhere to be seen.

Teddy sees Michael and Jason waving at us. They are the second half of our fearsome foursome.

Michael is a really talented artist and Jason is really good at sports. They are both really smart.

And we are all big fans of *Super Samurai from Outer Space*.

The show is about four Samurai brothers from ancient Japan. They come across a magical meteorite that crash-landed in their village. When they touch it, they transform into super warrior astronauts who can travel through the galaxy at the speed of light. Their new mission is to fight mutants and monsters trying to destroy the universe.

Sometimes that's exactly what being in third grade feels like!

"What's up, my Super Samurai bros?" I say, sitting at the table.

"Michael and I were just talking about the space project," Jason says. "We're going to be partners, and we're trying to brainstorm an idea."

"Awesome," I reply. "I'm teaming up with Teddy."

"Are you?" Teddy says, raising an eyebrow. "Just this morning you said you were going to chew me up and spit out my bones."

"YEESH," Jason says. "Just how hungry are you?"

"I was joking!" I said. "And that is only if I were a dinosaur."

"Ah, of course," Michael and Jason reply.

"Anyway, are you gonna be my partner or not?" I ask Teddy.

"Please, you know I am. I'll have to come up with a brilliant idea. I'm the brains of this operation," he says.

"More like the pain of this operation," I snap back with a grin.

We all laugh and open up our lunch boxes. This is where we compare snacks. If anyone has a not-so-tasty one, he tries to trade up for something better.

"An apple a day keeps the doctor away," I say.

I roll my apple into the middle of the table. I already know I want to trade it for Teddy's chocolate cookies, but I don't think he's going to let them go.

Michael rolls a giant grapefruit, and it bumps into my apple. Jason slides a handful of grapes toward the other fruit.

Teddy slowly pulls out his cookies and pushes them up against the rest.

"Oh, man, this stinks. I don't think I want to trade with any of you," he says.

I look down at the apple, grapes, and chocolate chip cookies. They are in a circle around the grapefruit, creating an amazing edible arrangement.

DING!

A lightbulb goes off inside my head.

"EUREKA!" I shout.

That's what the Super Samurai say on TV when they make a brilliant discovery. But I think a famous Greek scientist named Archimedes said it first.

"I just got an idea for our science project!" I add.

"What is it?" Michael and Jason ask.

"I'm not telling you guys because you'll want to copy it," I reply. "But I will say this one thing . . . it's going to be **OUT OF THIS WORLD!**" I wave my hands in the air like they are alien tentacles.

The girls at the table next to us stop talking and look at us.

"Can we help you?" Teddy asks.

"You guys are, like, so weird," one of them says.

I scoop a handful of grapes and shove them into my mouth until my cheeks are about to burst.

Then I smile at the girls.

It looks like I have grapes for teeth.

Teddy, Michael, and Jason laugh like hyenas while the girls roll their eyes and turn away in disgust.

I try to chew the grapes, but most of them pop out of my mouth and roll across the table. The guys laugh even more.

Suddenly a tall figure appears behind us. "What's
going on here?" she asks.

It's the lunch monitor.

Teddy quickly turns serious and says, "Uh, nothing, ma'am. We're just enjoying our lunch."

I manage to swallow and reply, "Yup! Everything's grape!"

My friends snicker and the lunch monitor scowls.

"I'm watching you," she says, giving each of us a look. **"ALWAYS. WATCHING."**

3
Edible Arrangement

I decide to tell Teddy my idea about the science project as soon as we go outside for recess.

"So what's the plan, man?" Teddy asks. "I'm dying to hear about your great project idea."

"Actually, it's a grape idea," I tell my friend.

I'm grinning from ear to ear.

"We are going to build a solar system out of food," I announce. "When I saw the fruit and snacks rolling around on the lunch table, it made me think of all the planets and moons and stars that orbit around each other out in space."

"Ha! That is a grape idea," Teddy says, laughing. "And certainly original. My brother made his model solar system out of painted Styrofoam balls and clay."

"Yeah, ours is going to be awesome *and* delicious," I reply. "And the best part is, if we mess up, we get to eat our mistakes!"

"It's a win-win situation, dude," Teddy says and gives me a high-five.

"I can't wait to go shopping for supplies," I say as I rub my tummy.

At the end of the school day, Teddy and I rush out to find my mom waiting in her car. Ruby is sitting in her car seat waving her hands. Then she pulls off one of her shoes and tries to eat it.

"Hi, Mom!" I say.

"Hi, Mrs. Burger," Teddy says.

He stays with us for a while after school sometimes until his parents get home and pick him up.

"Hello, boys," Mom says from the window. "How was your day?"

Teddy and I look at each other and say at the same time, "It was grape!" Then we laugh our heads off as we get into the car.

I tell Mom about the science project and ask her if we can take a trip to the supermarket to stock up on fruits and vegetables.

"Sure, honey," she says. "I have a few things that I need to pick up for dinner tonight, too."

"Cool. Maybe we can get some Astronaut Ice Cream, too!" I add. "As part of our research, of course!"

After we finish shopping, Teddy, Mom, Ruby, and I head back to the car with our groceries.

Along the way we pass this bakery called the House of Sweets. Sometimes Dad stops there in the morning for coffee and breakfast when he's rushing to work. And sometimes he brings us some treats after work, too.

The smell of donuts and cupcakes fills the air and I can't help myself. I need to go inside.

"Billy, where are you going?" Mom asks.

"Um, maybe we can use some donut holes and gumdrops and lollipops as props for our project," I say.

"Oh, yeah!" Teddy adds. "We can build a whole galaxy . . . if we don't eat it first!"

"Okay, fine," Mom says, handing me some money. "Make it fast, because we'll be in a world of trouble if Ruby doesn't eat dinner soon."

"Thanks, Mom!" I yell as Teddy and I run into the House of Sweets.

RING-A-LING! The little bell over the door jingles as we enter the store.

"Welcome, Billy and Teddy!" booms a big voice.

A small, round man with curly hair and a mustache appears from behind the counter. He is wearing a white apron covered in powdered sugar. It's Mr. Katisikis, the owner.

"You're just in time to meet my nephew Billy, who is visiting from Astoria with his friend Krystal. You are all around the same age, and two of you have the same name!"

A boy and a girl come out of the kitchen and wave hello to us.

Billy has glasses and is wearing a cool dinosaur T-shirt.

I like his style.

Krystal has curly black hair tied back with a glittery purple star-patterned scarf.

She's got some style, too.

"Nice to meet you," they say.

"Likewise," Teddy says and takes a small bow.

Krystal laughs.

"Mr. Katsikis," I say, "we need some ingredients for our solar system science project."

"Great galaxies!" Krystal exclaims. "I *love* the solar system! And I know all there is to know about it."

"Really?" I ask.

"Really," her friend Billy replies.

"Did you know that the solar system is made up of over one hundred worlds?" Krystal asks.

"I did know that!" I say.

"Did you know that some moons are actually larger than the planet Mercury?" she asks.

"I knew that!" Teddy says.

"Did you know that some moons, such as Io, have active volcanoes?"

"We didn't know that!" Teddy and I say together.

"Yup," Krystal states. "And the moon Titan has lakes, rivers, and oceans made of liquid methane!"

"P-U!" I say, holding my nose. "That's one gassy moon!"

Krystal laughs.

"Just like my friend Billy!" she says.

"Mine too!" Teddy says.

"SAY WHAT?!" I exclaim.

"Unlike the Billys, though, methane doesn't have a smell!" Krystal says.

"Good thing!" I say with a grin.

Suddenly a horn honks from outside. It's my mom, and she's signaling me to hurry up.

"Uh-oh," I say. "Looks like Mom's ready to blast off!"

4
Solar-System Smackdown

Teddy and I rush to the display counter and look at all the delicious treats.

"We'll take one of everything!" I shout and hand Mr. Katsikis my money.

The happy baker wraps the sweets neatly in a box. Then Teddy and I wave goodbye to Billy and Krystal and run out of the shop.

Mom is already halfway out of the parking spot, so we make a break for it.

Once Teddy and I settle in the backseat, we go over our sweet treats.

"There's gumdrops for moons and licorice swirls for the rings of Saturn and sprinkles for stars," I say.

"This is going to be the best science project in the entire history of Fork Lane Elementary School!" Teddy announces.

"Yeah, it is," I reply. "I can't wait to get started!"

As soon as we get home, Teddy and I rush into my room with the groceries and pour everything out on the floor.

I pull down a big book about space from my bookshelf and open to the solar system spread. We use it as a guide to help us separate our items into different groups.

A few minutes later, we have our basic solar system laid out on a large piece of wax paper from the bakery.

"Okay, let's go over what we've got," I say to Teddy.

"Roger that," he replies. "This big cantaloupe is going to be the Sun. Next, we have this cranberry as Mercury, an apricot as Venus, Earth is a plum, and Mars is a nectarine. Jupiter will be this grapefruit, Saturn can be an orange, Neptune is a green apple, and Uranus is a red grape."

"That's grape!" I say, and we both laugh.

"Oh, hey," Teddy says. "Where's Pluto? There was a blueberry right here!"

My friend points to an empty spot on the paper.

Suddenly we hear giggling behind us.

Teddy and I turn around to see Ruby sitting up and clapping her hands together. She has blueberry juice smeared all over her face and hands.

"Ruby!" I cry.

"Ruby!" my mom calls from the hall. "Where did you go?"

"She's in here, Mom!" I yell back. "And she's eating my homework!"

"That's a new one," Teddy laughs. "Sorry, Mr. Karas, but my baby sister ate my homework!"

Mom picks Ruby up and wipes her face and hands.

"Why don't we work on this at your house?" I ask Teddy. "It's much safer there."

"Good idea," Teddy says.

● ● ●

Teddy and I spend all weekend working on the project. We use a big cardboard box as a base for our diorama.

Teddy's dad helps paint it black in the backyard. Once it dries, we spray it with aerosol glue. Working quickly, Teddy and I drizzle the sprinkles onto the panels so that the space background is covered in stars.

"Now, on to the good stuff!" I say, wiping my hands of the extra sprinkles. "Let's moon our planets!"

"SAY WHAT?!" Teddy exclaims.

I pick up a gumdrop and a toothpick and show Teddy what I mean.

"First, we're going to stick the toothpicks in the fruit. Then, on the tip of each toothpick, we're going to stick a gumdrop onto it, see? Now it looks like the planets have moons orbiting around them."

"NICE!" Teddy says. "That's a great idea."

"Planet Earth has one moon named Luna, and Mars has two named Deimos and Phobos . . . so those are both easy." I tell my friend. "Jupiter, on the other hand, has sixty-seven moons!"

Teddy whistles.

"If we put that many toothpicks on the orange, it'll look like a pincushion!" he says.

Teddy's right, so he and I decide on the four biggest moons: Ganymede, Callisto, Io, and Europa.

We use something called goji berries for Jupiter's moons because they are slightly bigger than the gumdrops. They are also covered in chocolate. It's a good thing we're only doing four, because then we can eat the rest!

Once the planets are pierced with their moons, we lay them out in the circular pattern that matches my solar system book.

Teddy sticks plastic hooks onto the base of the diorama. These are going to secure our planets so they don't go rolling out of orbit.

While Teddy places the planets, I create the finishing touch: Halley's Comet!

I make it out of a lollipop, with licorice strings hanging from it to represent the tail. Then I loop a paper clip around it so it hangs it from a piece of thin wire stretching across the diorama.

"WHOOSH!" I yell, streaking the comet back and forth across the diorama.

Then Teddy and I stand back to admire our handiwork.

"Billy, this project is amazing!" Teddy says. "I bet Mr. Karas will be over the moon about it!"

I just smile with pride.

It's Monday morning and I jump out of bed and rush into the kitchen. Mom is feeding Ruby her oatmeal, and Dad is making breakfast.

"Shake a leg, everybody!" I cry. "Time for school!"

"I'm sorry, do I know you?" Dad says. "My son Billy hates Mondays, so you can't be him."

"Today's the big day!" I remind him. "Our science project is due! We need to get to Teddy's **ASAP!**"

"That's right," Dad says. He is taking Teddy and me to school on the way to the police station so we don't have to take the bus. This project is a masterpiece. It needs police protection!

Teddy is already waiting in the front yard with his mom when we arrive. They are holding the solar system, and together they slide it into the backseat of Dad's car. Teddy and I sit on either side, holding it carefully.

I ask Dad to turn on his police siren so we can roll up to school in style. He says no, but it was worth a shot.

Dad drops us off, and Teddy and I carry the project through the schoolyard.

Just then, Randy turns the corner. He sees us with our hands full and an evil smile curls across his face.

The bully quickens his pace and rushes toward us.

"Great, here comes trouble," I mumble.

Teddy and I scamper up the stairs as fast as we can but Randy catches up.

"Hey, nerds, what's in the bag?" he asks, blocking our path.

Teddy lets out a little whimper, but I'm not going to let him scare us. I muster up my courage.

"Just mind your own business!" I say.

I try to shove past Randy, but he grabs the bag and rips it off the diorama.

Randy pulls so hard that the project slips from our fingers.

"NO!" Teddy and I shout.

Teddy and I are frozen in place as our diorama hurtles through the air like Halley's Comet. It seems like it happens in slow-motion, like in a movie.

WHAM! BAM! CRASH!

We watch in horror as it smashes to stardust. Two days' worth of hard work is nothing more that a dirty fruit salad across the sidewalk.

"WHAT'S WRONG WITH YOU!?" Teddy shouts.

My friend overcomes his fear and turns red with anger. He shoves Randy, and the bully takes a step back. Then Randy laughs and pushes Teddy back, causing him to fall and scrape his knee.

I'm so angry I feel like I'm going to grow muscles and rip out of my clothes like the Incredible Hulk.

"AAAAARGH!" I shout.

I reach down and pick up what's left of the Sun and grab two handfuls of cantaloupe pulp. Then I lob them right at Randy's head.

WHOOSH!

"How about some slime balls for a slimeball?!" I shout.

Randy turns around and his eyes go wide.

The pulp explodes on impact—**SPLOOSH!**—covering Randy's head in sticky juice and seeds.

"We have contact!" I cry and cheer.

"Billy Burger!" booms a voice from the doorway. "My office . . . **NOW!**"

Oh, no.

It's Principal Crank.

He's standing at the door with his arms folded across his chest.

"Houston, " I say, "we have a problem."

5
Grounded

I follow Principal Crank back to his office. The hallways are starting to fill up with kids. They stare at me and whisper.

My face burns.

"This kind of behavior is completely and utterly inexcusable, Billy!" Principal Crank says.

Randy and I are seated in the two chairs opposite his desk. The bully is picking bits of cantaloupe out of his hair and shirt.

"Tell that to this guy," I reply, pointing next to me. "He started it!"

"NUH-UH!" Randy whines. "Your friend pushed me first. I was just defending myself."

"Gimme a break," I snap. "You're double our size, and you pick on us every day, because you don't think we'll fight back. Well, guess what, Buster. There's plenty more fruit where that came from!"

"Settle down, boys," Principal Crank says to us. "I think I've heard enough. I'm going to call your parents. Fighting on school grounds is a very serious offense. You are both suspended for the next two days."

"SAY WHAT?!" I shout in shock.

"Use this time wisely to think about what you've done and hopefully learn from your mistakes," Principal Crank states.

I slump back in my chair.

My parents are going to send me into orbit when they find out I've been suspended.

The rest of the morning goes by in a blur. Principal Crank calls my house and tells my mother to come pick me up. She is not happy about that.

"So, Billy, what do you have to say for yourself?" she asks me in the car.

I stare out the window at the trees whizzing by.

I replay the entire event in my head, and I don't see anything wrong with what I did.

"Randy was being a bully. He pushed Teddy and broke our science project, so I slimed that slimeball."

"I see," Mom says.

At work, my mother deals with really bad troublemakers all day at the police station. She tries to understand why they do what they do. That's why she is asking me questions instead of yelling at me.

"Do you think that was the right thing to do?" she asks.

"It felt like the right thing to do," I reply.

"I can understand that, honey. But most bullies act out because they are unhappy. They take out their anger on somebody else," Mom says. "I'm sorry about your project, but now you have to deal with the consequences of your actions. TV and video games are off-limits until further notice."

Oh no! I think to myself. *I'm gonna be SO bored!*

Mom pulls the car into the garage and shuts off the engine.

I drag my schoolbag into the house. Grandma is in the kitchen feeding Ruby, but I don't say hi to them. Instead, I head straight to my room. Then I shut the door really hard.

SLAM!

My Super Samurai action figures shake, rattle, and roll off the shelf.

Suddenly another door slams. Only this time, it's a car door and it's coming from outside.

I look out the window and see my dad stomping toward the house.

"Uh-oh!" I say.

6
In the Doghouse

"Suspension, William?" Dad hollers when he sees me. "I can't believe this. We don't allow fighting in this house."

"I wasn't fighting," I tell my dad. "I was defending Teddy from a bully who broke our project. He tried to hurt us." I look at him for a second. "Isn't that what you do at the police department?" I ask. "Protect people?"

Dad's expression changes. He doesn't look as mad.

"Well, yes, Billy, that's true. And I'm sure you were faced with a tough decision. But you know that you can count on teachers and the principal to help you the same way police officers do."

"I know that, Dad. It just . . . happened so quickly," I reply.

"I understand, but we still need to punish you," Dad says, putting an arm around me.

"Mom already says I can't watch TV or play video games for the rest of my life."

"Don't be so dramatic, Billy," Mom calls from the kitchen.

Ruby blows a raspberry in agreement. **PBBBBT!**

Grandma enters the room with Ruby and sits next to me on the couch.

"William, when you were a baby like Ruby, your grandfather and I took care of you together. He was a great man, who always led by example. He let his actions speak louder than words. In short, he was a model citizen," she says.

Grandpa was the first William Burger, but he passed away close to when Ruby was born about a year ago. I'm named after him, by the way.

"I want to be a model citizen just like Grandpa," I say.

Grandma smiles and pulls out a newspaper from her purse.

"My dear child, perhaps I can guide you in the right direction. It just so happens that there is an advertisement right here in the *Hicksville Illustrated*. The Shake-a-Paw Animal Shelter is looking for volunteers. How about you start there?"

"That's not a bad idea," Dad says. "Maybe something good will come out of this."

I start feeling a little better about the whole situation.

"Wonderful," Grandma says. "William can focus some of his energy into giving back to the community much like his grandfather. Why don't we head over there right now?"

"Why don't we get Randy to walk around town, scooping up dog poop, instead of me?" I reply.

"I'm sure he'll get what he deserves, too," Grandma says softly.

She takes me by the hand, and we head out of the house.

"William, your grandfather was a wonderful man: a loving husband and father and a decorated war hero," Grandma says as we walk down the block.

Usually, when I get in trouble, Grandma reminds me of all the good things Grandpa did that made him a model citizen. I get in trouble a lot, so Grandma ends up repeating herself a few times.

"Your grandfather helped the community in many ways. That is why that monument in the Hicksville town square is dedicated to him," Grandma adds. "And that is where we are going."

Right across the library and near the train station is a large fountain. It's the William Burger Reflecting Pool. (Says so right on a marble sign at the base.) It really is a neat fountain, and I visit it with my family all the time.

The Hicksville town square is a few minutes away, and I don't mind the walk. It's so nice out, I almost forget why I'm not in school.

Then I remember, and I feel a little sad.

When we get to the fountain, Grandma sits on the edge and rubs her fingers along the sign. The monument is a round pool made of polished black stone, with three jets of water shooting into the air.

The wind sprays drops of water into my face.

"Your grandfather fought for his country and protected the lives of friends, family, and strangers. You have the same spirit. So does your father. That's why you want to protect and help people."

"Yes! That's why I stood up to Randy!"

"Boys like Randy probably need someone to be nice to them," Grandma says.

"Are you saying I should be his friend?" I gasp.

Grandma smiles.

"Then I shouldn't be a dog walker, I should be a lion tamer!" I exclaim.

● ● ●

After Grandma's brief rest, we walk inside Shake-a-Paw. There is a young woman with blond hair at the front desk. Her name tag says Julie G.

"Hi there, how can I help you?" she asks.

Grandma gives me a nudge, and I step forward.

"Hi, I'm Billy," I say. "And I'm interested in volunteering."

"Wonderful!" Julie says.

The young woman comes around the counter and hands Grandma a sheet of paper. "Would you mind filling out some paperwork in the meantime?"

"I don't mind at all," Grandma says.

While Grandma writes, Julie says, "Now, Billy, usually volunteers your age start with simpler tasks, like helping me around the office."

SAY WHAT?!

I thought I was going to walk dogs and be outside and play fetch and have fun. Not work in an office.

This was a terrible idea!

7
Friends
Fur-ever!

Julie leads me across the room to a wall lined with cat cages.

"One of your tasks will be to help me clean the cat cages, including the kitty litter!"

I scrunch my face and Julie laughs.

"It's not so bad," she says. "The cats are really friendly, and they like it if you rub their bellies and scratch behind their ears."

Julie takes my hand and rests it on the head of a smooth gray cat named Ella.

Ella closes her eyes and purrs happily. Maybe Julie is right. This kind of office work isn't so bad!

BARK! BARK! BARK!

Suddenly our attention turns to three barking dogs coming out of a back room. The cats in the cages jump and hiss.

With the dogs is a teenager wearing a bright blue T-shirt and holding three leashes.

The dogs hop and jump and wag their tails at the sight of Grandma and me. They run around the teen until his legs are tangled in the leashes. They look like furry moons orbiting a big planet!

Julie says, "This is Billy, and he's here to lend a hand!"

"Hey, Billy," says the teen. "I'm Joe. And you have perfect timing. I could certainly use a hand . . . or two . . . or three!"

Joe hands me one of the leashes, but Julie stops him.

"Billy is brand-new, and he's not ready to go dog walking just yet," she says.

The white and brown dog hops up to sniff me and wags his tail. I pet his head and rub behind his ears.

"This Jack Russell Terrier is named Astro," Joe says,

"He's really friendly," I say.

"Astro is very temperamental. He doesn't like that many people, but he's a good judge of character. You must be a really good person, Billy," Joe says.

"Well, I'm trying to be!" I say.

Joe introduces me to the dogs he is holding. "These two are Rooney and Emma. Rooney is a French bulldog, and Emma is a pug. I was just about to take the whole gang out for a walk so they could sign Nature's guest book . . . if you know what I mean," Joe says with a wink.

I laugh.

"You mean the dogs are going out to pee!" I explain.

"Is it okay if I tag along with Joe?" I ask Julie. "I really wanted to be a dog walker, so I'll just watch and see how it's done."

Julie thinks for a moment. "Okay, but just watch," she says finally.

YES!

"See ya," I yell over my shoulder as I follow Joe out the door.

● ● ●

Astro is full of energy and he yips and barks at everything and everyone that passes. He stops to sniff the parking meter, the fire hydrants, and the garbage cans.

"This is super exciting," I say to Joe. "I really love animals, but we can't have a pet because my dad is allergic."

"Ha, that's funny," Joe replies. "That's the very same reason I got a job at the shelter. I love animals, but I can't have one, either!"

Joe is a really cool guy. And he's my first friend who is an actual teenager!

When we get to the edge of the block, Astro bolts toward the fountain.

"YAAAH!" Joe shouts as he's pulled through the square.

"What's with him!?" I ask, running after them.

"It's time to do his business," Joe says. "Astro likes going right here under the fancy bushes around this fancy fountain."

"Really?" I exclaim. "This fountain is dedicated to my grandpa for being a model citizen. And dogs use it as their **BATHROOM?!**"

"Well, at least these dogs have good taste," Joe says, handing me a plastic bag.

I scrunch my nose as the smell of Astro's "business" fills the air.

"It's a dirty job, but somebody's gotta do it, Billy," Joe says. "You wanted to be part of the team. Well, welcome aboard!"

Joe shows me how to pick up the poop by sliding my hand inside the plastic bag and wearing it like a glove. Then he shows me how to turn it inside out, trapping the waste inside, and tying the top in a tight knot.

As quickly as possible, I clean up Astro's poop. It's warm and stinky and squishy. I can't wait to throw it in the nearby trash can.

I guess Emma and Rooney got jealous, because they both do their business, too!

Joe cleans up after them, and we continue to walk back to the animal shelter.

We walk along the other side of the street. This time it's my turn to follow my nose, and I smell the sweet aroma of fresh donuts coming from the House of Sweets.

Mr. Katsikis is placing a piping-hot tray of gooey, delicious glazed donuts in the window. Without thinking, I press my face against it. Astro does the same, and we both have a little bit of drool sliding down the sides of our mouths.

"Billy, when did you get a dog?" Mr. Katsikis asks.

"I didn't. I'm helping out at the shelter!"

"You're a good boy. Your family must be very proud. I know if you were my son, I'd be proud, too!" the baker says.

It felt really good to hear Mr. Katsikis say that. I have a big smile on my face as I continue to walk Astro.

Joe and I pass Mr. Roeser's Little Shop of Flowers, as well as Jingles & Jokes Jamboree.

"SAY WHAT!?" I cry. "The joke shop is always closed when I get home from school, but I'm not in school today! Can we go inside?"

"Yeah, this place is awesome," says Joe. "The owners are two really nice ladies named Mary-Kate and Natalie."

"I can't wait to buy some of that gum that turns your teeth black when you chew it. I'm gonna trick my friend Teddy!"

Just as we approach the joke shop, Astro goes the opposite direction. His snout is pointing at Nice to Meat You, the butcher shop. He tries to run in, but Joe tugs his leash to pull him back.

"Are ya hungry, boy?" he asks Astro.

Astro hangs out his tongue and sits. Joe pulls out a doggie treat from his pocket, and Astro chomps it up in seconds.

"Good boy," Joe says and pets Astro's head.

Then he turns to me.

"This furball is a fireball," Joe says. "Once he gets going, he's faster than a speeding comet!"

I nod my head and follow Joe back to the animal shelter.

Grandma spots me and smiles.

"How did it go?" she asks.

"It was a blast!" I say. "I can't wait to do it again tomorrow."

"Wonderful!" Julie replies. "Come by around noon."

"Make it twelve-thirty," I say. "I need to eat lunch first. I can't walk dogs on an empty stomach!"

8
Unleashed!

The next morning I wake up and look out the window. It is a beautiful sunny day. Then I remember that I don't have to go to school. It feels like a vacation day!

Only it's not.

Dad left a list of chores for me to do around the house as part of my punishment. On top of the list it says: "This is **NOT** a vacation day."

The list reads:

CLEAN YOUR ROOM.

SWEEP THE GARAGE.

SORT OUT THE RECYCLABLES

TAKE OUT THE TRASH.

By the time I've taken care of everything on the list, I look up at the clock in the den.

"Good gravy!" I exclaim. "It's almost lunchtime!"

I quickly change my clothes and run into the kitchen.

Grandma is in there feeding Ruby because Mom and Dad are both at work. Ruby is spitting out green peas onto her bib and then smearing her hands in them. She thinks it's the funniest thing in the world.

Grandma greets me with a "Good afternoon, William."

"Good afternoon, Grandma," I reply. "What's for lunch?"

Grandma smiles and kisses me on the forehead.

"You must have worked up quite an appetite. There are sandwiches on the counter. Help yourself and then we'll get ready to head to the animal shelter."

"MMMM!" I say as I bite into one. It's turkey and Swiss cheese on whole-wheat bread with extra mayo. There's some spinach in there, too.

I'm gonna need all the energy I can get. This volunteer stuff is hard work!

After Grandma places Ruby in her stroller and straps her in, we head out to the Hicksville Shopping Center.

Grandma drops me off at the animal shelter and kisses me good-bye. Then she takes Ruby to the playground across the street.

I kind of want to go to the playground, too, I think, *but I'm on a mission to be a model citizen.*

I enter the shelter and wave hello to Julie.

She smiles and waves at me from behind the desk. But she is talking on the phone and writing things down on a piece of paper.

"Hey, big guy!" Joe says when he sees me. "Ready for round two?"

"I was born ready!" I say, following him into the back room.

There is a loud chorus of barks and howls when the dogs see me.

"They're always happy to get visitors," Joe says.

Together, Joe and I start our tasks of cleaning cages and brushing the dogs and feeding them before we take them out for walks.

When Astro sees me, he wags his tail and barks hello. I pet him on the head and rub his ears while he licks my face.

"Hey, Astro," I say. "It's nice to see you, too!" He's probably getting all the leftover mayo on my face.

When Astro notices the leash in Joe's hand, he barks even more.

"Looks like this furball is ready to roll," Joe says.

Then he winks at me.

"Hey, Billy, you think you're ready to walk Astro?"

SAY WHAT?!

"I was born ready!" I say.

This is going to be **AWESOME**.

I can't believe Joe is trusting me. I tell myself to be cool, but I'm really excited. My heart is beating fast. I really want to do a good job and impress Joe.

"Walking Astro is a big responsibility, but I have faith in you," Joe says.

I guess Astro agrees because he jumps up and tries to lick my face.

"Let's go!" I say.

We wave goodbye to Julie, but she doesn't look up from her work.

Then we take the usual path down the block past all the stores. The dogs do their usual thing and stop and sniff everything.

At the end of the block, Astro sees the William Burger Reflecting Pool—also known as his bathroom. He starts barking and tugging me forward.

"I think Astro is ready to do his business," I tell Joe.

"Okay, big guy," he says to me. "These two are stopping to smell all the roses. So run along and meet me back here when he's done, okay?"

I nod my head yes and look both ways before crossing the street. It feels kind of cool and grown-up to be doing this on my own.

Astro is super excited to be in his favorite part of the town square. He takes two laps around the fountain before settling down to do his poo.

Once I scoop the poop, I tie the plastic bag and bring it to the trash can on the corner.

"Hey, Billy!" calls a voice from behind me.

I turn around to see Teddy and his dad.

"Whoa!" I exclaim. "Hey, dude. What are you doing here?"

"School's out for the day, man," Teddy answers. "And my dad wanted to get some coffee at the House of Sweets. I didn't think I'd see you out in public for another twenty years."

Teddy's dad waves at me as he walks into the bakery.

"Wow, I didn't even realize what time it was," I tell him. "Guess time really does fly when you're having fun."

"Fun? I just saw you scooping up dog poop!" Teddy cries, pointing to the trash. "That stinks!"

Astro barks at Teddy.

"Sorry, dog, but it does!" Teddy says to Astro.

"Hey, it's a dirty job, but someone's gotta do it," I say. "Meet Astro. He's my new four-legged friend."

Astro sits on his hind legs and extends his paw.

Teddy shakes it and then pulls out a cell phone from his pocket.

"I'm glad I found you because I have some amazingly awesome news to tell you."

Teddy's grin goes from ear to ear.

"What is it?" I ask. "Did Principal Crank retire?"

"Ha, I wish!" Teddy says. "Check this out."

He scrolls through the pictures on his dad's phone. He stops on some photos of our solar system project sitting in the garage before we brought it to school. Before Randy ruined it.

"It turns out my dad took pictures and video of our project with his phone after he helped us put it together," Teddy tells me.

I stare at my best friend in surprise.

"COOL!" I say. "Now we can always remember it!"

"That's not even the best part," Teddy explains. His grin is so wide now it looks like his head might flip inside out.

"I showed them to Mr. Karas today. He thought they were awesome. We got an **A+** on the project!"

"SAY WHAT!?" I yell at the top of my lungs.

Astro barks at all the noise.

"Dude!" I exclaim. "That is epically awesome!"

"I KNOW!" Teddy cries.

He raises both his hands for a double high-five.

I'm so excited that I drop Astro's leash to high-five Teddy.

SLAP! SLAP!

And right at that very moment, a fuzzy gray squirrel sprints across the ledge of the fountain. Astro barks at the little critter, scaring it off the fountain.

The squirrel darts into the bushes and disappears from sight.

The dog bolts after it and also disappears.
"OH, NO! ASTRO!" I cry. "He's gone!"

9
Search Party

"ASTRO!" I shout, searching through the shrubs. "ASTRO, WHERE ARE YOU?"

Joe comes running from across the street with Emma and Rooney in tow.

"What happened?!" he asks.

"I dropped the leash by accident, and Astro ran away!" I answer. "I'm so sorry!"

Joe pats me on the shoulder. "Okay, listen up, big guy. We gotta act fast. The square is small enough to search if we all work together. But Astro could get hurt if we don't find him soon."

The teen looks at the phone in Teddy's hand.

"Give me your number, kid. I'll send you a picture of Astro. We can both show it around to people," Joe says.

"Yes!" I cry. "We can start a search party like they do on the police force!"

While Teddy and Joe exchange numbers, Teddy's dad and Mr. Katsikis come out of the House of Sweets.

"What's going on here?" asks Teddy's dad.

Teddy shows him the phone. There's a picture of Astro, sitting up near the fountain. "We're looking for this lost dog. Can you help us?"

"Of course!" Mr. Katsikis replies. "Send that photo to my phone, and I will share it with others, too."

"Awesome," I say. "Thanks so much. If we split up, we can cover more ground to find Astro!"

"I'll go with you," Teddy says. "I think I saw him go that way!"

Teddy and I run toward the park behind the fountain.

Just then, Mr. Roeser comes out of his store as Mary-Kate and Natalie exit theirs. We nearly collide into each other!

"What is all the hubbub?" Mr. Roeser asks us.

"No time for chatting, Mr. Roeser," I tell the florist.

Joe runs up behind us with Emma and Rooney.

"You guys go on ahead," Joe replies. "I can explain. Hurry!"

"Thanks, Joe," I yell over my shoulder as Teddy and I run into the park.

My friend and I turn in a full circle, scanning the area for any sign of Astro. There are lots of grown-ups eating their lunch on benches and tables and lots of really little kids playing on the playground.

"No sign of Astro," I say.

"Maybe we need a better view," Teddy says. He points to the big slide.

"Great idea," I exclaim. "That's why two heads are better than one!"

I rush over to the slide just as a mom and her toddler are about to use it.

"Pardon me," I say, "but this is an emergency. We're on the hunt for a lost dog!"

I push past them and climb to the top of the slide. "I don't think he's up there," the mom says to me.

From where I'm standing, I can see over the park and most of the square. I see Teddy's dad and Mr. Katsikis searching on the left side of the shopping center. Mary-Kate and Natalie search on the right.

Joe has returned Emma and Rooney to the shelter and is now searching the middle area of the square with Julie.

I shield my eyes from the sunlight and focus on a brown blur moving quickly through the trees at the edge of the park.

The blur runs through a clearing, and I get a better view. It's Astro!

His leash trails behind him like a comet's tail. And he's heading for a familiar part of the shopping center.

"Target spotted!" I shout down to Teddy. "I know where he's going!"

"Where?" Teddy asks.

"NICE TO MEAT YOU!" I shout.

Teddy looks puzzled. "It's nice to meet you, too, man. But we've been best friends for years. Did the sun fry your brain up there? Did you lose your memory?"

"No!" I yell, climbing down the ladder. "*Nice to Meat You* is the name of the butcher shop. That's where Astro's going! I'm sure of it!"

Suddenly someone else blocks my path.

What is it with all these people popping up out of nowhere? I say to myself.

"Excuse me," I say, trying to pass. "I'm on a mission!"

"Merciful heavens, William Burger!" says a stern voice. "Just what is going on here?"

I look up to see Grandma holding Ruby.

"Grandma, I lost Astro!" I explain. "I tried really hard to be responsible but I messed up again. Now I'm doing my best to make things right. To be a model citizen!"

I run past Grandma and Ruby toward the opposite end of the park.

Teddy follows right next to me.

We quickly look both ways before crossing the street. The butcher shop is all the way at the end of the block. Astro is weaving in and out of pedestrians' paths to get there.

Then an idea hits me.

"Teddy, you run to the front of the store. I'm going to cut through this alley and come around from behind. That way we can corner Astro and grab him before he gets away!"

"AYE, AYE, CAPTAIN," Teddy says and takes off.

I'm sweating really hard and breathing heavy, but I push myself to run faster. I reach the alley and dart around the dumpsters and piles of garbage.

All of a sudden—**THUD!**

This time I crash into another person and fall backward onto my behind. **"OUCH,"** I yelp.

"Watch it, loser!" says the person in front of me.

"Oh, great," I gulp. "It's Randy the Savage!"

10
Billy Burger: Model Citizen

I'm trapped in the alley with Randy and he's pounding his fist into the palm of his hand.

"What . . . what . . . are you doing here?" I stammer.

"That's none of your business, **DWEEB**," Randy sneers.

I get up off the ground and walk backwards, searching for an escape route.

"I'm not looking for trouble, Randy. I'm just looking for a lost dog," I say, holding my hands up.

"And I'm looking to rearrange your face," Randy threatens. "There's no principal here to save you this time."

CLANG!

I back into a trash can and catch myself from tripping over it.

Reaching inside, I pull out a rotten head of cabbage.

"Stay back, Randy," I shout. "I don't want to fight you, but I will defend myself!"

"HA!" Randy laughs, pointing at the vegetable in my hand. "With what . . . that? This is going to be easier than I thought."

Just as Randy cracks his knuckles and takes a step closer, a loud barking shape bounds down the alley and leaps onto his back.

WHAM!

It's Astro!

My new furry best friend tackles the bully to the floor. "Aw, yeah, Astro!" I cheer.

Randy scrapes his hands and knees and whimpers in pain. Astro pins Randy down with his front paws and barks in his face.

WOOF! WOOF! WOOF!

Randy grimaces and starts to cry. I'm shocked to see him act like such a big baby.

"Get him off me! Get him off me!" he shrieks.

"WAAAAAAAAH!"

I pull Astro by the collar and get him to settle down by patting his sides and rubbing his ears. Then I grab his leash and loop it around my wrist twice so I don't lose him again.

"Good boy, Astro," I say. "I'm so glad you came back! Good boy!"

I look down at Randy. His sobbing makes me feel a little sorry for him. Maybe Grandma was right. Maybe he just needs a friend.

I use my free hand to help him up off the ground. He eyes me suspiciously and then he takes it.

"Are you okay?" I ask.

"Yeah," Randy sniffs, wiping his eyes.

Then he mutters, "Thanks. Please don't tell anyone I was crying."

At that very moment, Teddy comes running around the corner into the alley.

"Billy, what's going on?" he shouts. "I heard screaming!"

Then he freezes in his tracks when he sees Randy.

"Don't start with me, you bully," Teddy shouts, balling his fists. "Or I'll knock your block off!"

"Teddy, it's okay," I say, putting myself between the two of them. "You see, Randy . . . uh . . . he helped me find Astro."

"SAY WHAT?!" Teddy exclaims.

"Yeah, it's true. If it weren't for Randy, I wouldn't have found Astro."

Teddy lowers his fists and shakes his head.

"I don't understand what's happening. This is Randy the Savage we're talking about here!"

"I know, man. It's hard to believe," I say, looking at Randy. "But let's just say his bark is worse than his bite."

Randy smiles a little.

"I'm sorry for picking on you," he says.

Teddy's eyes go wide.

"None of this makes sense," he says, shaking his head. "I must be dreaming. Am I sleeping? Pinch me, Billy. Pinch me."

I laugh and give him a soft pinch. "Maybe this is a dream," I say. "Or maybe it's time we give Randy a chance to be our friend."

Teddy still looks suspicious. "That sounds more like a nightmare."

"Look at it this way. If Randy tries one of his old tricks again, we have a four-legged bodyguard to take care of business."

"Now we're talking," Teddy says.

Astro barks in agreement and leads the way out of the alley back onto the main street.

Teddy, Randy, and I follow. When we turn the corner, we see Joe and Julie sprinting up the block.

"Hey, everyone!" Joe shouts. "They're over here!"

Mr. Katsikis, Mr. Roeser, Teddy's dad, Grandma, Ruby, Mary-Kate, and Natalie quickly surround us. They clap their hands and cheer.

"Way to go, Billy," Joe says. "You found Astro!"

"Actually, Astro found me," I tell the teen. "I really tried to be a good volunteer. But I guess I messed up a little, huh?"

"Don't be so hard on yourself, kid," Joe says, patting me on the back. "The good news is, Astro is safe and sound. And the better news? You brought us all together!"

Joe turns to look at all the people surrounding us.

"He's right!" says Mary-Kate. "Even though we all work in the same shopping center, we didn't really know each other until today."

"Indeed," adds Natalie. "Before we were just neighbors, but now we're all friends!"

"And we have you to thank, Billy Burger," says Mr. Roeser.

"Whoa!" I exclaim. "I don't know what to say."

"Say 'thank you,' dear," Grandma tells me.

I thank everyone for their kind words.

Then I think, *Is this what it's like to be a model citizen?*

"Ahem," Randy says, clearing his throat. He looks at Joe. "Do you have room for one more volunteer?"

"Maybe you should stick with playing with the kittens for a while, until you get over your fear of dogs, that is," I say.

Randy's cheeks turn red, but he smiles.

"Make that two volunteers!" chimes Teddy.

"Wonderful," replies Julie. "The more model citizens the merrier! Follow me to the shelter, and we'll get you signed up."

"Billy, my sweet child," Grandma says, "your actions were inspirational! Young people like you make our community a better place. I know your grandfather would be proud of you because I am very proud of you."

I give her a hug, and she kisses my head.

Then I hand Astro's leash over to Joe. "Do you mind taking Astro back without me? I want to go home and tell my mom and dad all about what happened."

"Sure thing, big guy," Joe says. "You've got quite the tale to tell."

"It was certainly an adventure," I say. "Not only was it out of this world . . . it was **ASTRO-NOMICAL!**"

About the Author

New York Times best-selling author John Sazaklis enjoys writing children's books about his favorite characters. He has also illustrated Spider-Man books and created toys used in *MAD Magazine*. To him, it's a dream come true! John lives with his family in New York City.

About the Illustrator

Lee Robinson grew up in a small town in England. As a child, he wasn't a strong reader, but the art in books always caught his eye. He loved to see how the characters came to life. He decided to become an illustrator so he could create worlds of characters himself. In addition to illustrating books and comic books, Lee runs workshops to help teach kids about literacy, art, and creativity through comics.

Billy's Glossary

consequences—things that happen after you do something; Most grown-ups only use the word *consequences* when you do something bad

constellations—special groups of stars with certain names, like Orion and the Big Dipper; Imagine if there was a Billy Burger constellation

diorama—a special project you do for school that's a model of something bigger

dissect—to take something apart, piece by piece; In the case of a frog, you get to cut it open first

edible—if it is edible, it means you can eat it, and you know I will

emergencies—super serious problems where people or things could really get hurt

inspirational—inspirational things make you want to act a certain way, like the Super Samurai make me want to be epically awesome, just like them

galaxy—a super huge group of stars and planets; Our galaxy is the Milky Way, which honestly makes me a little hungry

gazelle—fast animals that sort of look like deer with two awesome horns; Gazelles live in Africa and Asia and in zoos

meteorite—a piece of rock or metal from space that falls to Earth

mutants—people or animals that change from their normal form into monsters, like me when I am super hungry

mythology—a collection of awesome stories about gods and warriors and heroes

offense—wrongdoing, misdeed, crime, rule-breaking . . . you get the idea

suspended—kicked out of school for a few days or even longer

suspicious—unsure you can trust what's going on; I might still be suspicious of Randy for a while, even if we are trying to be friends

technicality—a tiny little detail that might not mean much to most people

temperamental—if you are temperamental, you get upset easily; I'm usually only temperamental when I'm hungry

universe—everything in space; We're talking the planets, stars, moons . . . you get the picture

Ken is a nine-year-old boy living in the southern Philippines. For as long as he could remember, he dreamed of helping the stray animals he saw on the streets. He wanted to open an animal shelter, but he figured it would take many years to reach his goal. In the meantime, he gave the animals food and spent time with them.

But in 2014, photos of him with some dogs spread all over the Internet. People from all over the world sent him money! He was able to pay for veterinarian care and better food. Then his dad helped him set up a small shelter in their garage, until so much money was donated, he was able to open a larger shelter. The shelter is known as the Happy Animals Club.

On the Happy Animals Club website, Ken explains, "The dogs are not kept in cages unless they are ill or there is some other good reason. The cats have a very big living area solely for them. **ALL OF THE DOGS AND CATS AT HAPPY ANIMALS CLUB ARE VERY HAPPY ANIMALS!"**

Ken and his shelter help the animals get healthy and gain weight, since most of them are underweight. The animals also learn to not be scared of people. Once they are ready, people in the Philippines can adopt them.

To help Ken and the Happy Animals Club, you can donate money to the shelter at www.happyanimalsclub.org